Dear Parent:
Your child's love of reading starts here!

Every child learns to read in a different way and at his or her own speed. Some go back and forth between reading levels and read favorite books again and again. Others read through each level in order. You can help your young reader improve and become more confident by encouraging his or her own interests and abilities. From books your child reads with you to the first books he or she reads alone, there are I Can Read Books for every stage of reading:

SHARED READING
Basic language, word repetition, and whimsical illustrations, ideal for sharing with your emergent reader

BEGINNING READING
Short sentences, familiar words, and simple concepts for children eager to read on their own

READING WITH HELP
Engaging stories, longer sentences, and language play for developing readers

READING ALONE
Complex plots, challenging vocabulary, and high-interest topics for the independent reader

ADVANCED READING
Short paragraphs, chapters, and exciting themes for the perfect bridge to chapter books

I Can Read Books have introduced children to the joy of reading since 1957. Featuring award-winning authors and illustrators and a fabulous cast of beloved characters, I Can Read Books set the standard for beginning readers.

A lifetime of discovery begins with the magical words "I Can Read!"

Visit www.icanread.com for information
on enriching your child's reading experience.

I Can Read Book® is a trademark of HarperCollins Publishers.

Batman: Reptile Rampage
Copyright © 2012 DC Comics. BATMAN and all related characters and elements are trademarks of and © DC Comics. (S12)
HARP 2515
Manufactured in China. No part of this book may be used or reproduced in any manner whatsoever without written permission except in the case of brief quotations embodied in critical articles and reviews. For information address HarperCollins Children's Books, a division of HarperCollins Publishers, 10 East 53rd Street, New York, NY 10022.
www.icanread.com

Library of Congress catalog card number: 2011938184
ISBN: 978-0-06-188521-1
Book design by John Sazaklis

12 13 14 15 16 SCP 10 9 8 7 6 5 4 3 2 1   ❖   First Edition

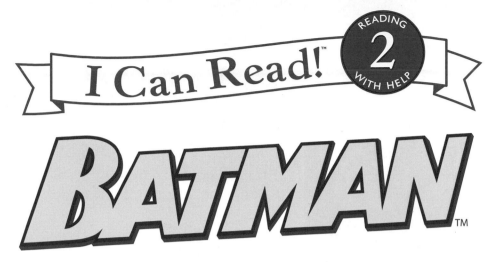

BATMAN ™

Reptile Rampage

by Katharine Turner

pictures by Steven E. Gordon

colors by Eric A. Gordon

BATMAN created by Bob Kane

HARPER

An Imprint of HarperCollins*Publishers*

BRUCE WAYNE

Bruce is a rich businessman. He trained his body and mind to become Batman, the Caped Crusader.

TIM DRAKE

Tim is in high school. He is smart and athletic. He is also Robin.

COMMISSIONER JAMES GORDON

James W. Gordon is the head of Gotham's police department and a close friend of the Dark Knight.

BATMAN

Batman is an expert martial artist, crime fighter, and inventor. He is known as the World's Greatest Detective.

ROBIN

Robin is Batman's partner and sidekick. Together they keep Gotham City safe. Robin is also known as the Boy Wonder.

KILLER CROC

Waylon Jones was once a circus strongman. Now, as a result of a rare skin disease, he is a sewer-dwelling criminal with mutated reptilian features.

Batman is in the Batcave

when he sees the news.

A famous doctor has been kidnapped.

Batman takes the Batmobile

to the doctor's office.

As soon as he sees the evidence,

he knows who is behind this crime.

"Killer Croc," Batman tells the police.

Batman watches a security tape

from the doctor's office.

"Where is the antidote?" Croc yells.

"I don't have it here," the doctor says.

"It's at Gotham General Hospital."

Commissioner Gordon tells
the staff to clear the hospital
while Batman sets his trap.

As night falls over Gotham,
a dark figure sneaks into the hospital.
"This is too easy," Croc says
as he takes the antidote.
But when he turns to leave,
he finds himself face-to-face with Batman.

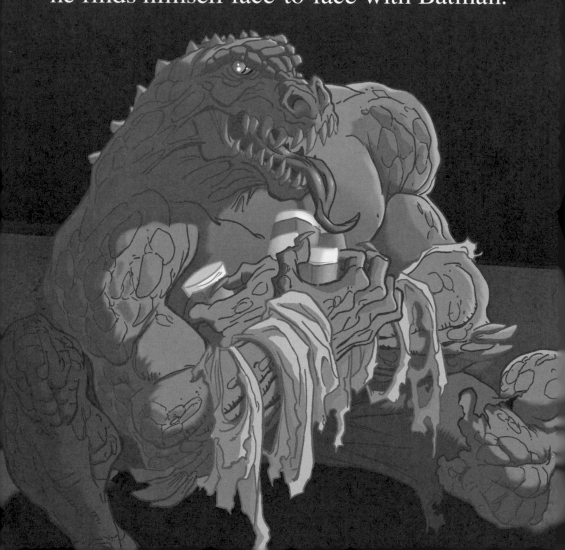

"Do you have an appointment?"
Batman asks.

"Batman," Croc growls,

"get out of my way."

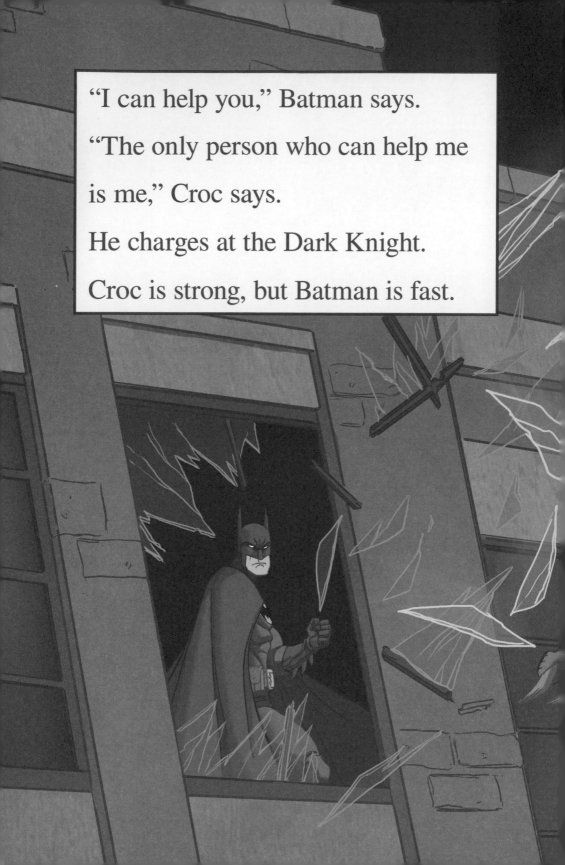

"I can help you," Batman says.

"The only person who can help me is me," Croc says.

He charges at the Dark Knight.

Croc is strong, but Batman is fast.

Batman moves out of the way,
and Croc crashes through a window.

Croc lands safely on the street below.

He looks back once

before disappearing into the sewers.

"You let him get away!"

Commissioner Gordon says to Batman.

"No, I didn't," replies Batman.

He holds up a small screen

showing a flashing red dot.

Batman had hidden a tracking device

on Croc's scaly skin.

"He'll take us right to the doctor."

"How will you follow him in the sewers?"

asks the commissioner.

"I can help with that," says a voice.

Robin stands in the doorway.

He is holding two scuba suits.

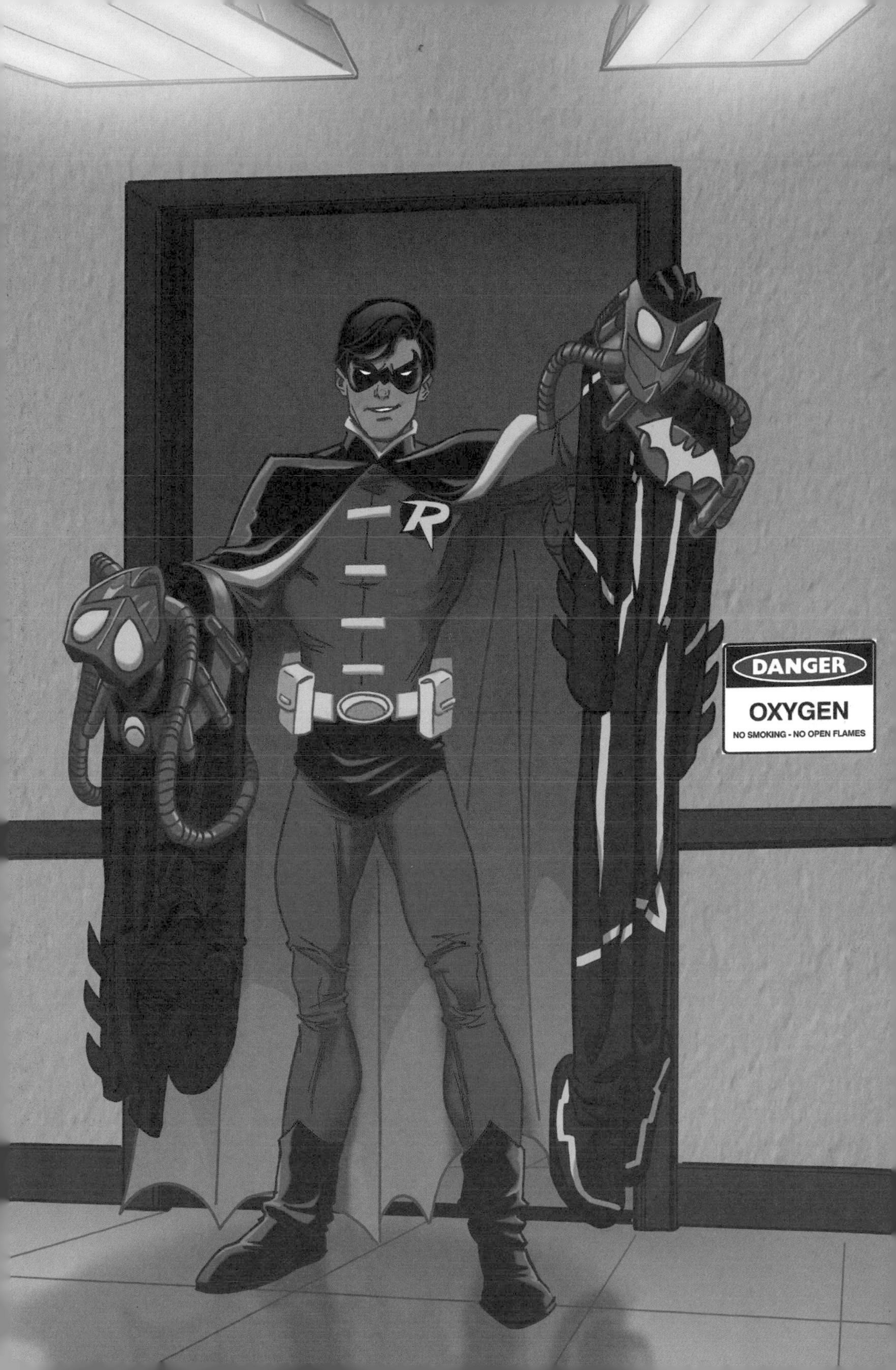
DANGER
OXYGEN
NO SMOKING - NO OPEN FLAMES

Soon, Batman and Robin are swimming

through the sewers after Croc.

The red dot finally stops moving.

They have found Croc's hideout.

The Dynamic Duo sees

the missing doctor tied up inside.

"I'll untie the doc," Robin whispers.

"You stop the Croc."

Croc is mixing the antidote

he stole so he can cure himself.

"It ends now," Batman says.

Croc whirls around.

"Batman!" Croc says.

"You're just in time for dinner.

My pets are very hungry!"

Suddenly, two crocodiles

swim out of the sewer water.

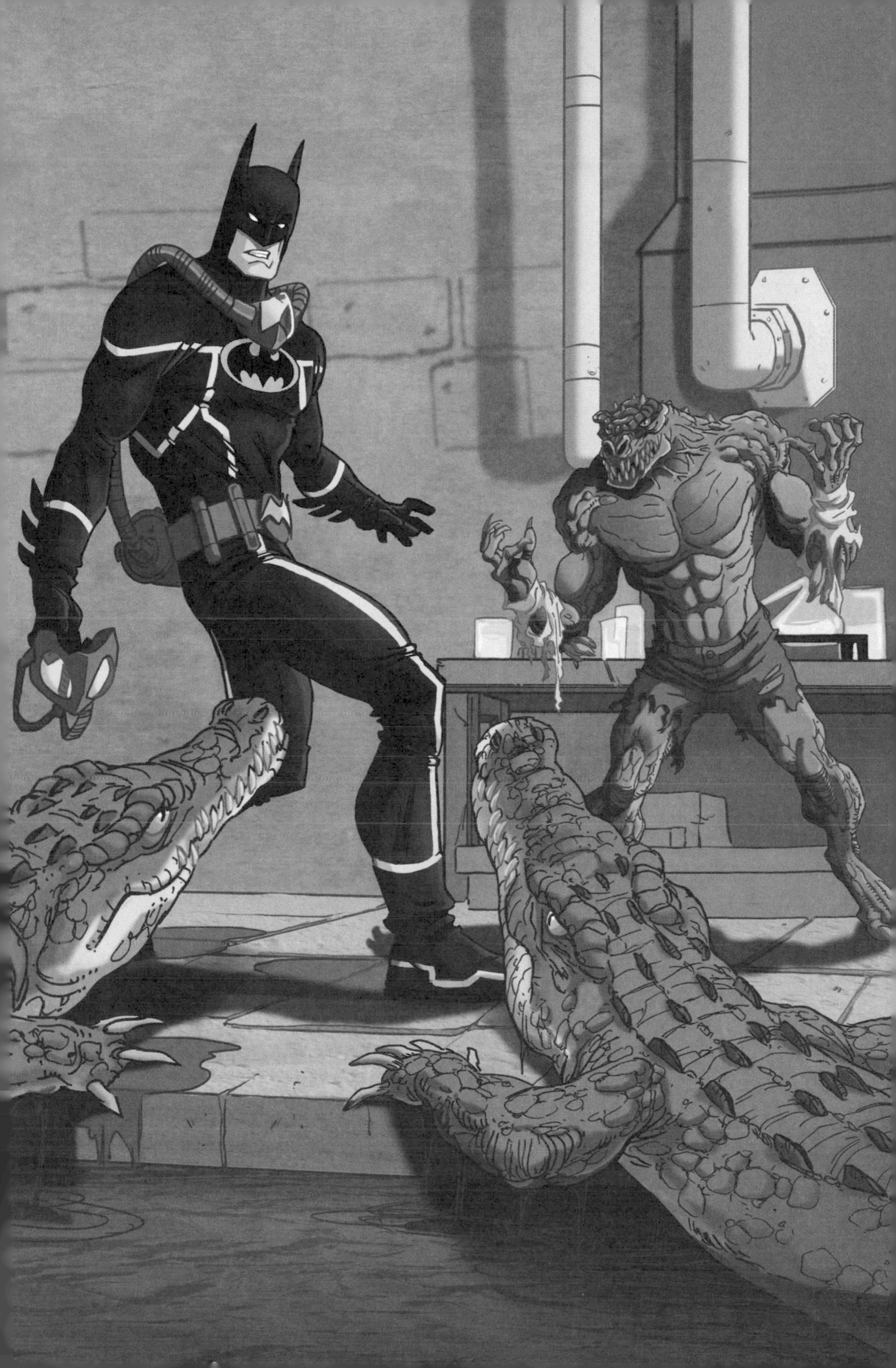

The crocs are on top of Batman
in an instant.

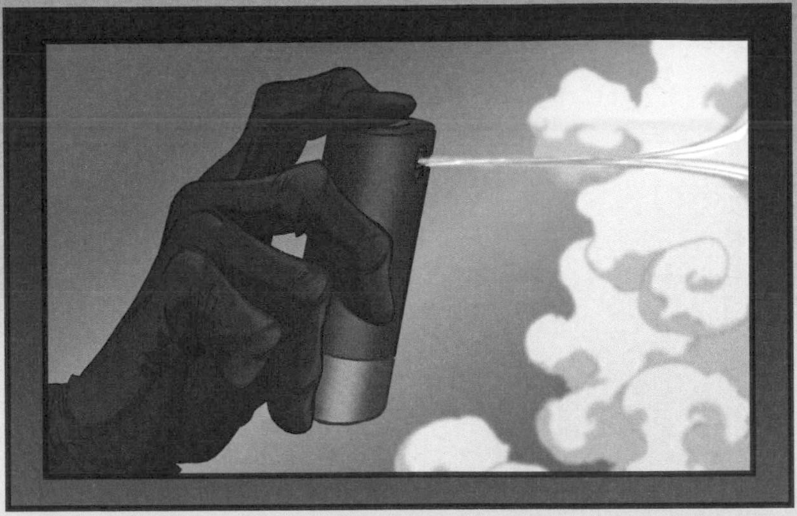

He reaches for the reptile repellent
in his Utility Belt.
Batman sprays the beasts
and they quickly fall asleep.

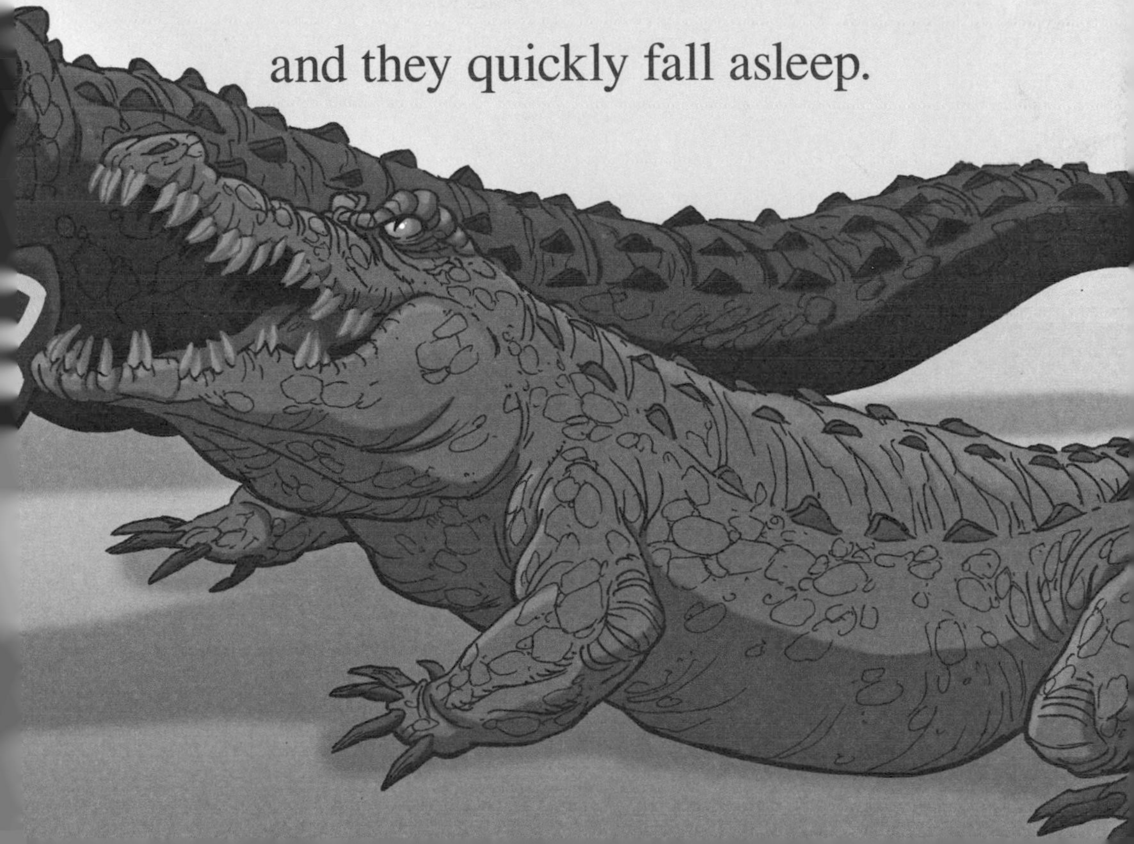

Batman catches up to Croc just in time.

"You can't beat me, Batman," Croc cries.

"I'm here to help you," Batman says.

"There are good doctors in prison."

"No one's ever helped me before.

Why would they start now?" Croc yells,

and lunges at Batman.

But the Caped Crusader is ready.

The pair wrestles to the ground.
Batman fights to keep himself
out of Croc's jaws.

Robin grabs Croc's antidote.

"You want this, Lizard Lips?" Robin says.

"Come and get it!"

"No!" Croc screams

and dives in after the bottles.

Batman makes sure the doctor is okay before he and Robin dive in after Croc. Croc finds the bottles and then discovers he's not alone.

The Dynamic Duo realizes that they can't beat Croc with strength alone. Batman signals to Robin to split up.

Killer Croc makes a quick choice.

He follows Robin.

He thinks the Boy Wonder

will be easy to catch.

30